STORIES FROM BRAMBLY HEDGE

WILFRED
TO THE RESCUE

Atheneum Books for Young Readers

An imprint of Simon & Schuster Children's Publishing Division

1230 Avenue of the Americas

New York, New York 10020

Copyright © 2005 by HarperCollins Publishers Ltd.

First published in Great Britain in 2005 by HarperCollins Children's Books

The text of this book is set in EdGoudy.

The illustrations are rendered in watercolor.

Manufactured in China

First U.S. edition 2006

CIP data for this book is available from the Library of Congress.

ISBN-13: 978-1-4169-0901-9

ISBN-10: 1-4169-0901-X

WILFRED
TO THE RESCUE

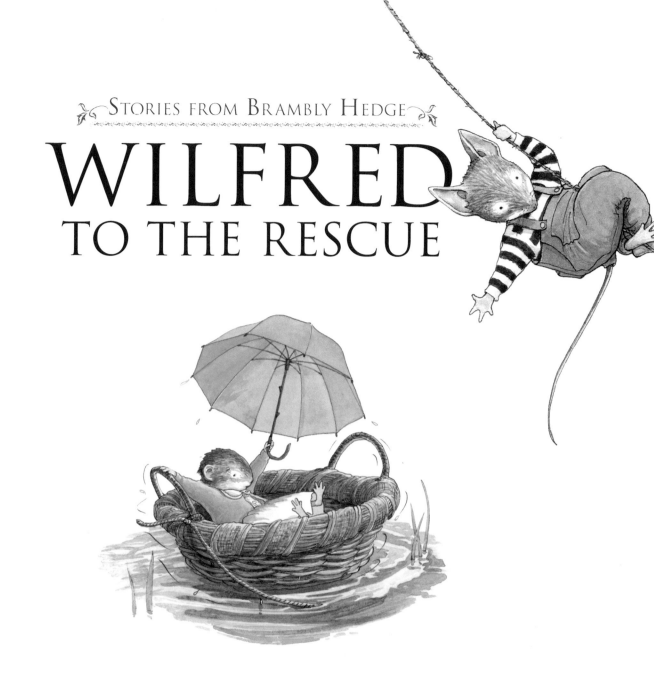

Written by Alan MacDonald · Illustrated by Lizzie Sanders

Based on the world created by Jill Barklem

Atheneum Books for Young Readers
New York London Toronto Syndey

It had been raining for three days and three nights in Brambly Hedge. Wilfred's friend, Primrose, had come over to play.

"Rain, rain, rain," Wilfred grumbled. "Is it ever going to stop?"

That night it rained even harder. . . .

When Wilfred and his dad went out the next
morning, they stared in astonishment.
"Where's the field gone?" Wilfred asked.

"By my whiskers! The water's almost up to the house,"
said his dad. "The stream must have burst its banks."

After breakfast, Wilfred sploshed over to Primrose's
house. He found her watching as a basket boat
was unloaded.

"It's the Voles," explained Primrose. "Their
home is flooded, and they've got
nowhere to stay."

The Vole children
were called Horace
and Sissy.

"Are you going to
sleep at our house?" Primrose asked.

"Dunno," Horace shrugged.

Primrose's dad said that everyone
would stay with them until the
flood went down.

Wilfred helped to fetch food supplies from
the Store Stump on his dad's raft. They brought back
blackberry buns, cheeses, and hazelnuts.

That evening they all crowded into the dining room
for a wonderful feast.

Later, Primrose suggested playing
a game of Hide-and-Squeak.
"Mind you look after Sissy," Mrs. Vole told Horace.

While Horace counted to ten, everyone ran
off to hide. "Coming—ready or not!"
called Horace excitedly.

Horace found Wilfred and Primrose quite easily.
"But I can't find Sissy anywhere," he said.
"We'll help you look," offered Wilfred.

Sissy had found the perfect hiding place in the basket boat, under her mom's green umbrella. For a long time she waited. The boat bobbed gently on the water, making her sleepy.

Suddenly Sissy woke up. The boat seemed to
be moving. Peeping out, she saw that the rope
had come loose. The boat was drifting.
"Mo-om!" Sissy cried, but the wind
carried her small voice away.

Back at the house, Horace, Wilfred, and Primrose had searched every room.

"She's run off!" said Horace crossly.

Wilfred was staring outside. "That's odd," he said. "Where's your boat gone?"

Horace turned pale. "Do you think Sissy took it?"

Horace ran and hid under the bed and wouldn't come out. "Go away!" he said.

"But what about Sissy? She could be in trouble!" urged Primrose.

Wilfred tried to think. "You could take the raft. She couldn't have gone far."

"Will you come too, Wilfred?" asked Horace in a small voice.

Primrose reluctantly agreed to stay behind in case Sissy turned up.

As dusk fell, Wilfred pushed the raft off from the landing. Muddy water swirled around them. Wilfred steered while Horace called, "SISSY!" into the gloom.

Alone in the boat, Sissy clung to her mom's umbrella. She could no longer see the warm lights of the house. She was cold and lost. The current made the boat spin dizzily.

An old weeping willow trailed its branches in the water.
As the boat drifted by, Sissy tried to grab hold.
But she leaned out too far. The boat tipped
and—SPLASH!—she tumbled over the side.

Meanwhile, Horace and Wilfred's throats
were sore from calling Sissy's name.

Wilfred pointed at something on the water.

"Look! What's that?"

"Mom's umbrella!" said Horace.

"See if you can reach it."

As it bobbed past, Wilfred managed to catch the
umbrella and draw it in. Something was curled up inside:
a small, wet ball of fur. It blinked at them in surprise.

"Sissy!" cried Horace.

Back at the house Primrose had explained
everything. Mrs. Vole cried so much that
she needed to borrow three hankies. Outside in
the dark, tiny lanterns searched up and down.
"Look!" cried Primrose. "A light on the water!"

The light drew closer until, finally, they could see the raft.
On it were Horace and Sissy, with Wilfred steering them
safely home. A great cheer went up from everyone.

A little later they all ate toasted crumpets
around the kitchen fire. Horace told everyone that
he was probably the bravest vole in the world.

Wilfred bit into another crumpet. "The thing about
rescuing," he said, "is it makes you very hungry."